Wild Wings

Poems for Young People by **Jane Yolen**

For Elizabeth — Fly high!
Jane Yolen 2002

Photographs by

Jason Stemple

Wordsong § Boyds Mills Press

To all the Stemple bird watchers, but especially David — J. Y.

To my father, for passing down his love of birds — J. S.

Text copyright © 2002 by Jane Yolen
Photographs copyright © 2002 by Jason Stemple

Published by Wordsong
Boyds Mills Press, Inc.
A Highlights Company
815 Church Street
Honesdale, Pennsylvania 18431
Printed in China

U.S. Cataloging-in-Publication Data
(Library of Congress Standards)
Yolen, Jane.
Wild wings : poems for young people / by Jane Yolen ;
photographs by Jason Stemple.—1st ed.
[32]p. : col. photos. ; cm.
Summary: Birds in the wild are captured in photographs and poetic form.
ISBN 1-56397-904-7
1. Birds—Juvenile poetry. 2. Children's poetry, American.
I. Stemple, Jason. II. Title.
811.54 21 2002 CIP AC
00-106799

First edition, 2002
Book designed by Jason Thorne.
The text of this book is set in 18-point Garamond.

Visit our Web site at www.boydsmillspress.com

10 9 8 7 6 5 4 3 2 1

Front cover: broad-tailed hummingbird (Selasphorus platycercus)
back cover: snow geese (Chen caerulescens)
page 1: anhinga (Anhinga anhinga)
page 4: red-shouldered hawk (Buteo lineatus)

Contents

A Note from the Author

My son Jason Stemple and I are part of a family of bird watchers. My husband—the real-life Pa in my book *Owl Moon*—taught us all. Our three children used to play bird-identification games from the car as we traveled around the countryside.

As soon as each child was old enough to handle field glasses, she or he was given a pair. Being the youngest, Jason received his binoculars last. But he was always the keenest birder of the family. When he was eight years old, an influx of great gray owls came down from the Arctic into our little Massachusetts town. Jason would get on his bicycle and ride the two and a half miles to the place where a pair of the great grays was regularly seen. There he would watch for hours, even helping adult bird watchers spot them.

Today Jason, with his field glasses and his telephoto-lens camera, is still bird watching. After a long trip to observe wildlife along the South Carolina shore and in the Florida Everglades, he sent me a batch of bird photographs: ibis, heron, anhinga, moorhen with alligator. "More!" I said to him. I knew I had to write poems for those pictures.

So he took more photos in Colorado: hawk, vulture, a yak with blackbirds. I was flooded with his wonderful photographs, images of a variety of birds I have tried to capture in lyric lines.

You can do it, too.

Egret

A cloud of feathers
above the feathered pond,
an eye that does not see
beyond

      the fish at its feet,
      the food in its beak,
      the fear in its throat,
      the man in the boat.

A rush of broad wings,
cloud to sky,
no time to think.
Good-bye.

A favorite of plume hunters, the great egret (Ardea alba) *has long decorative feathers (aigrettes) that adorn it only during breeding season. When the egret majestically flaps away, it carries its long neck folded, head between the shoulders. Its long legs extend behind like a rudder.*

Moorhen with Gator

On a riverbank
a sleepy alligator
waits like a long
parenthesis
as a single moorhen
passes below.

Oh, to be so
unsuspecting,
part of
that brief moment
before
the sentence in the water
is finished
with a brutal
punctuation.

*The common moorhen, or common gallinule
(Gallinula chloropus), is a ducklike bird that can be
found swimming in freshwater marshes as well as in
ponds and placid rivers. It also likes to wade in the
reeds. When it swims, it pumps its head and neck.*

Wilson's Warbler

As if sunshine
fell down on a branch,
then gathered itself together
for one solid moment,
the warbler brightens spring.

Wilson's warbler (Wilsonia pusilla), *like
many warblers, is a small, brightly colored bird.
The males are the singers. These warblers
especially love to perch in willow thickets.*

11

Vulture

High above, black angel wings
Make halos in the sky.
But on the ground, a graveyard beak
And hunger in the eye.

The turkey vulture (Cathartes aura) *is a common bird
whose great, wide, circling pattern of flight is elegant and
elliptical. Close up, though, the bird is grotesque, for it
is a carrion eater with a massive and terrifying beak
needed for its scavenging work.*

Anhinga after Swimming

Imagine wet shirt,
An invisible line,
Shoulder to shoulder
Across the damp spine.

The wind swiftly blowing
Until the shirt's dry,
You put it on slowly—
Then—take off and fly.

The anhinga (Anhinga anhinga)
is a common bird found in freshwater
swamps, marshes, ponds, and lakes.
A fish eater, it often swims with only
its snaky neck and head exposed.

14

Heron in the Grass

Snaking through the reeds,
wary and wise,
searching for food
through marble eyes:
frogs, eels, tadpoles,
an occasional herring,
the heron moves
with quiet daring.

The great blue heron (Ardea herodias) *is a voracious eater. Besides the frogs, eels, tadpoles, and herring mentioned in the poem, the great blue heron has been known to devour salamanders, lizards, birds, shrews, meadow mice, young rats, aquatic insects, moths, butterflies, grasshoppers, and dragonflies.*

Swallows: A Haiku

They decorate trees,
White breasts candled from within:
Ornaments of spring.

The violet-green swallow (Tachycineta thalassina), *like other swallows, is a strong, elegant flier. Found in western North America, it nests in holes in trees and in the crevices of rocky cliffs.*

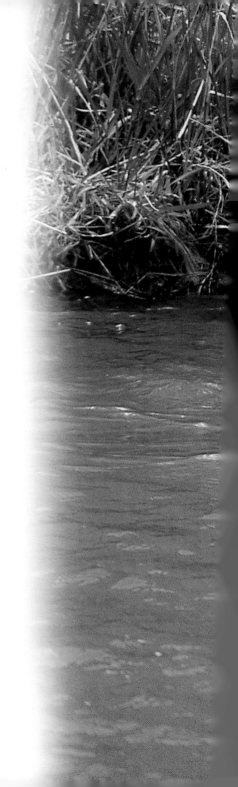

Swimming Lesson

Think of the river, part water, part sky,
Think of the downy mother
Teaching her goslings not only to fly
But—by putting one webbed foot
                              in front of the other—

To swim right across the rippling waves,
For *that's* how a proper young gosling behaves!

The Canada goose (Branta canadensis) *is the most common and probably
the best-known goose. It breeds on lakeshores and in coastal marshes. When it
migrates, the goose flies both day and night. Its honking call is very familiar.*

Brother Hawk

Why wait upon that solitary perch?
I search
for tiny shrews beneath dry grass,
for mice who, gray and silent, pass
and think they have escaped my eye.
And then I fly.

What do you think of the air?
I care
that wind can tickle all my feathers,
that wings, despite the fickle weathers,
will always give me one flight more.
And then I soar.

The red-shouldered hawk (Buteo lineatus) *is one of the most common hawks of eastern North America. It often hunts from a perch, looking for rodents, insects, and small birds. The red-shouldered hawk is one of the soaring hawks that circle the sky, then drop precipitously on their prey.*

Green Heron

Fancy that—
Reed acrobat
Balancing upside down
On a brown pole.

*The green heron (Butorides virescens),
also called fly-up-the-creek, actually
looks more blue than green. It is found
near small ponds and streams, where
it feasts on minnows, insects, larvae,
crayfish, and even snakes.*

25

Tree of Life

In what soft Eden,
under a golden sky,
do silver-white birds
on a shadow tree
preen themselves?
You call them ibis, but I
believe they are the souls
of our lost dead—parents,
grandparents,
great-grandparents—
those we knew, and those who came
before we could know them.

The white ibis (Eudocimus albus) *is abundant
along the Gulf Coast of the United States, where
it nests at night in large tree rookeries.*

Landscape with Yak and Birds

Grazing between brown splotches,
the yak considers the landscape.
So what if it hasn't the soul of a painter,
it certainly enjoys the green.

Blackbirds grazing beside it
are but small, dark stains;
tubed paint squeezed onto the green canvas,
now a smudge of wings,

                              then gone.

The yellow-headed blackbird
(Xanthocephalus xanthocephalus)
is commonly found on farmland,
where it congregates with other
types of blackbirds.

Hummer

Brief moment of a bird,
hovering for a heartbeat by a flower,
pausing between raindrops,
between sun patches,
between one thought and another,
your stay is shorter than this poem.

The broad-tailed hummingbird (Selasphorus
platycercus) *is a western bird whose wingbeats
are so fast they produce a loud, harsh whistle.
Hummingbirds are the smallest of the
North American birds.*

Marsh Sunset

Photo finish:
wild wings stilled,
a solitary anhinga
takes its roost.
Who could resist
such a shot,
a study in reds and black
and silence.